KT-561-941

Pennie the pinkest polar bear

Sarah Phillips · Stuart Lynch

make
believe
ideas

Pennie's a friendly polar bear,
but she is very, very shy.
She stammers as she says her name
and often starts to cry.

She blushes pink from head to toe
and can't think what to say.
Who wants to play with a PINK bear?
So she usually runs away.

"You need to keep your **throat** **warm** with something **woolly** and **thick!**" says **Dan.** "My bark is **always** clear. This **scarf** will do the **trick.**"

"Now let's **stretch** and **twist** our necks and try some **short**, sharp **sounds**."

So they **cough** and **bark** and stand up **tall** and **wind** their **heads** around.

Later on a **cool** new **cat**
comes **sauntering** down the **street.**
Pennie runs up to say **hello,**
but **stammers** and retreats.

Cool Cat's shocked
but understands.
She knows just what to do.

"Come and drink
my special milk.
It'll soothe your
throat for you."

Pennie and Cool Cat sip the milk,
warmed and mixed with honey.
They even try some "singing",
but Dan doesn't find that funny!

As Pennie runs back through the park,
she meets the Treetop Twins.

"H-h-hi, I-I'M P-P-P-....!" she stammers
before escaping to the swings.

The Treetop Twins
know how to help.
They say, "We have no doubt
if you learn to say our
tongue-twister,
it will sort the
stammering out!

Just then the travelling pigs arrive
with big bags and a ball.
"H-hi, I'm P-P-P-...!" Pennie cries,
before her tears begin to fall.

"Come with us," the kind pigs say,
"Let's **all** have some **fun**.

We'll **dance** and **sing** together,
and **join** the others **later** on!"

"Pink is the perfect colour!
That's what we both say.

Enjoy the fact that you turn pink
and hope to stay that way!"

As the **moon** shines in the **sky**
and **stars** start to **twinkle,**

the hushed friends inside the tent
hear silver bells that tinkle...

In comes Pennie,
dressed in pink.
She does a dance,
and sings,
"I'm Pennie the
pinkest polar bear,
and I want to say
these things:

You're very welcome to the show.
We hope you enjoy it all.
There's dancing, music, acrobatics
and a very special ball!"

Pennie sits down, pink as pink,
and smiles at all her friends.
She's wowed by the amazing acts
and loves the mice at the end.

Pennie is walking home with Dan;
they're dancing as they go.

"Pink is the perfect colour –
I want everyone to know!"

Don't be **cross** with how you are.
Enjoy yourself and **see**
that the **More** you gain in **confidence**,
the **happier** you'll be!